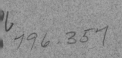

DISCARD

THEY
SHAPED
THE
GAME

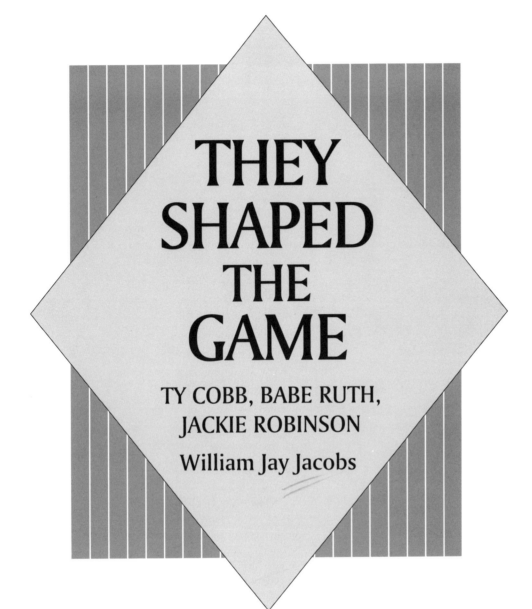

THEY SHAPED THE GAME

TY COBB, BABE RUTH, JACKIE ROBINSON

William Jay Jacobs

CHARLES SCRIBNER'S SONS · NEW YORK
Maxwell Macmillan Canada · Toronto
Maxwell Macmillan International
New York · Oxford · Singapore · Sydney

Charles Scribner's Sons Books for Young Readers
Macmillan Publishing Company
866 Third Avenue, New York, NY 10022

Maxwell Macmillan Canada, Inc.
1200 Eglinton Avenue East, Suite 200
Don Mills, Ontario M3C 3N1

Macmillan Publishing Company is part of the
Maxwell Communication Group of Companies.

First edition   10   9   8   7   6   5   4   3   2   1
Printed in the United States of America

Library of Congress Cataloging-in-Publication Data
Jacobs, William Jay.
They shaped the game / William Jay Jacobs. — 1st ed.
p.   cm.
Includes bibliographical references and index.
ISBN 0-684-19734-0
1. Baseball players—United States—Biography—Juvenile literature.
2. Cobb, Ty, 1886–1961—Juvenile literature.
3. Ruth, Babe, 1895–1948—Juvenile literature.
4. Robinson, Jackie, 1919–1972—Juvenile literature.
[1. Baseball players. 2. Cobb, Ty, 1886–1961.
3. Ruth, Babe 1895–1948. 4. Robinson, Jackie, 1919–1972.] I. Title.
GV865.A1J33 1994   796.357'092'273—dc20 [B]   94-14007

Summary: Profiles of three players who affected the course of baseball history

Dedicated to the memory of Yankee pitching great Waite Hoyt, a teammate of Babe Ruth. As a baseball broadcaster in Cincinnati, he helped to shape the values and worldview of young people, along with a sense of what life is all about.

—W. J. J.

Lives of great men all remind us
We can make our lives sublime.
And, departing, leave behind us
Footprints on the sands of time.

—HENRY WADSWORTH LONGFELLOW

CONTENTS

PREFACE

William Shakespeare, not surprisingly, probably was the one to put it best. He once wrote: "Be not afraid of greatness. Some are born great, some achieve greatness, and some have greatness thrust upon them."

Babe Ruth, almost certainly the outstanding home run hitter in baseball history, also won high honors as a major league pitcher. Clearly, Ruth was a gifted athlete—one "born" to greatness.

Ty Cobb inherited far less ability. Yet he played the game with almost animal-like passion and fierceness, and with a mean, aggressive spirit. Perhaps as a result, he compiled a lifetime batting average of .367, an achievement that may never again be equaled. His was the accomplishment of a man who "achieved greatness."

Jackie Robinson had "greatness thrust upon him." It was Robinson who, after many decades of prejudice, became the first black athlete allowed to play in the major leagues. Still, if he had lacked either the natural talent of an exceptional ballplayer or the driving zeal—the "will"—to succeed, then baseball history might indeed have been very different.

Robinson cleared a pathway for the outstanding black athletes of today.

It is no accident that, many years ago, when the Baseball Writers of America chose the first five players to be inducted into the Baseball Hall of Fame at Cooperstown, New York, the largest number of votes cast went to Ty Cobb, with almost as many for Babe Ruth.

Nor is it surprising that, in the years since World War II, the name that stands out most boldly in writings about baseball history is Jackie Robinson.

Cobb, Ruth, and Robinson—three vastly different kinds of men, with vastly different styles of personal existence. Yet the three of them stand high, indeed at the very pinnacle of baseball greatness.

Because of that, there is much to learn from them about the game of baseball, about the achievement of greatness, and about the experience we all share in a broader game—the game of life.

TYRUS RAYMOND ("TY") COBB
(1886–1961)

Courtesy of National Baseball Library & Archive, Cooperstown, New York

August 8, 1905. Pretty Mrs. Amanda Cobb lay asleep in her bedroom. Suddenly she was awakened by a noise on the porch roof outside. Frightened, she reached for the double-barreled shotgun near her bed. Pointing the gun toward the window, she fired twice. Then, looking out into the darkness, she saw a body.

There, in a pool of blood, lay her husband, Professor William H. Cobb, who had told her he would be away for the night.

The tragedy of that event did much to shape the world-view of the couple's son, eighteen-year-old Tyrus Raymond Cobb. Young "Ty" was destined to become perhaps the greatest—and certainly the most angry and aggressive—player in the history of professional baseball.

Ty's father had hoped for his bright young son to choose a career other than baseball, preferably medicine or the military. Little could he predict that the already fiery youngster would become, for that era, the game's highest-paid performer.

Nor could he know that Ty would establish records during his career destined to last for many decades, including, for example, 4,191 lifetime hits and 96 stolen bases in a single season. Most astonishingly, Cobb won twelve American League batting championships—nine of them in a row. Where one player recently led the American League in hitting with an average of .301, Ty Cobb compiled a lifetime average of .367. For twenty-three years he batted over .300, including eleven consecutive years at an average of .368 or higher.

Meanwhile, by using his high salary to buy stock in Coca-Cola and other companies, Cobb became a multimillionaire.

In the eyes of many Americans, Cobb had everything: fabulous wealth, a reputation for baseball greatness, an attractive family including several children, and a healthy body that would keep him alive well into his seventies.

Yet surprisingly, despite all of those clear-cut marks of success, Ty Cobb was destined to live a life filled with deep unhappiness.

To the very end of his existence he was known as a man who hated blacks—sometimes striking at them with his fists or with a weapon. Both on and off the ball field he often argued viciously with players on other teams—and his own team— even coming to blows with them.

When running the bases he assumed that the base paths belonged to him and that those who stood in his way deserved to be the targets of his highly sharpened spikes. Long after a particular game ended he sometimes would carry on bitter personal conflicts, arranging to fight in a hotel room or on the street.

Still, there is no question that Ty Cobb's achievements mark him as one of baseball's greatest players, perhaps the greatest of them all.

Cobb was born on December 18, 1886, in a small community in rural Georgia. His ancestors included doctors and lawyers. Cobbs had been prominent military leaders in the American Revolution, while two served as Southern generals in the Civil War.

Cobb sliding into third base. Cobb believed the base paths belonged to him. Anyone who stood in his way was a doomed target for his spiked shoes. *Courtesy of National Baseball Library & Archive, Cooperstown, New York*

Cobb's father named him Tyrus after the ancient city of Tyre, whose citizens had stood bravely against the mighty Alexander the Great in the fourth century B.C. Such fierce resistance, according to the older Cobb, truly was the mark of manliness.

As a student, young Tyrus disappointed his father. Although very bright, he seldom stood out academically, convinced that he never could be the equal of so outstanding a parent. Instead he turned to the sport of baseball as a way to rival the achievements of his father.

At the age of fourteen Ty threw himself into competition with well-developed athletes eighteen to twenty-five years old. Equipped with only a tattered old baseball glove for that struggle, he sold two of the fine books in his father's personal library, using the money to buy a new glove that he adored.

The senior Cobb responded with a firmness that his son would never forget. Yet, even that early in life, young Ty found it crucial to stick to a path once he had started the journey. He kept the glove.

By the time he was seventeen years old, Ty Cobb had come to a decision: He would become a professional baseball player. His father responded with deep anger, demanding that he go to college and then engage in "real work."

One night, father and son argued until three o'clock in the morning. Soon afterward, as Cobb later remembered it, the elder Cobb declared to his son, "So long as you're in it now . . . Tyrus . . . go after it. . . . And one thing more—don't come home a failure!"

Many years later, after becoming very famous, Cobb remembered that his father, by giving him such a blessing to go on, had made him totally determined to succeed.

At first, serving as an outfielder for the Augusta, Georgia, professional ball club, Ty experienced only mixed success. But, even that early, big league scouts knew of his reputation for wildness and for daring. Often he stretched singles into doubles. He stole base after base. Sometimes he would try to go from first base to third on a simple sacrifice bunt. One scouting report described him as "the craziest ballplayer I ever saw."

By the end of August 1905, Cobb had joined a major league baseball team, the Detroit Tigers.

But it was just before then, on August 9, that he received word of his father's bloody death. No other event in his life would prove so devastating to him. Nor would the bitterness ever fade from his memory.

Intelligent, intense, already known for his speed on the base paths, Ty Cobb soon registered his first base hit as a member of the Tigers. In the many years to follow he added over four thousand more hits. Along with them would come a national reputation that surely would have impressed even his father, a man not easy to please.

In the early twentieth century the task of trying to get started in professional baseball could be difficult for almost any ballplayer. But for Ty Cobb, an aggressive young Southerner angered by his father's death, the beginning proved to be a serious challenge. To Cobb it became not just a test of his ability, but of his character.

Detroit Tiger players once sawed Cobb's personal baseball bats in two. They locked him out of the team's bathroom in a hotel. They threw soggy newspapers at him.

According to "Wahoo" Sam Crawford, a Tiger outfielder at the time, Cobb took the hazing in the wrong way. Instead of just laughing at it all, like other rookies did, the young Southerner was "still fighting the Civil War." He thought the Northerners were all against him, trying to punish him as a "Rebel."

As a result, he fought back—both on the field and off—trying to prove that he was the best man around. The "old-timers," he said, turned him from a "mild-mannered Sunday School boy" into "a snarling wildcat."

Before long Cobb's professional ability won out, making

ıormously successful. But very soon, too, he became the
ıated man in the major leagues.

ccording to Cobb, he simply came to understand that
ıanners his family had taught him "had no place in baseball." Or as he put it, "I knew I'd have to forget being a gentleman and show them that I was rougher and tougher than
any of them."

Despite his great success on the field, particularly as a
base runner and hitter, Ty Cobb usually found himself alone
after the day's ball game was over. Without friends, he stayed
to himself.

For hours at a time he would read in public libraries or
visit museums and art galleries. He came to enjoy operas and
concerts, hearing the works of such classical figures as
Beethoven, Brahms, and Chopin. Meanwhile his readings
about two of history's most powerful figures, Julius Caesar
and Napoléon, turned them into his special heroes—and
models for his own conduct.

By the spring of 1908 Cobb had become convinced that
baseball truly should be his life career. His Detroit Tiger teammates, although still not friendly to him, no longer hazed him.
In that year he eventually captured the American League batting championship. He also had won a reputation for daring
baserunning, as well as for sliding hard into infield defenders,
his spikes sharpened and high.

In early August of the 1908 season Cobb announced to
his manager that he was leaving the team for a while. Why?
To be married.

Traveling to Georgia, the twenty-one-year-old Ty Cobb
married Charlie Marion Lombard, a seventeen-year-old girl.
Returning quickly to Detroit with his young bride, he played

an important role in helping the Tigers capture the American League pennant.

For Cobb success in baseball soon became an avenue leading him to important contacts. On one visit to the nation's capital to play against that city's team, the Washington Senators, the Tigers all were introduced to President William Howard Taft. So impressed was the president with Ty Cobb's intelligence and charm that on several occasions in the next few years he arranged to play golf with the young baseball star.

On the ball field, however, Cobb was anything but charming. Once, he dragged a bunt down the first-base line, knowing that the pitcher, who purposely had thrown at him, would cover the bag. After making the putout at first the pitcher ran well into foul territory. Still Cobb leaped into the air with spiked shoes flashing. He ripped his victim's uniform and, as a lesson, succeeded in thoroughly frightening him.

At about that same time, Connie Mack, the manager of the Philadelphia Athletics, who many years later would become Ty Cobb's friend and defender, called him the dirtiest player in baseball history.

Not in his youth—nor ever afterward—was Cobb's temper limited to the playing field. In September 1909 he took offense at the words of a black elevator operator-watchman in Cleveland, slashing him with a knife before finally being stunned by the man's nightstick.

Sometimes, too, Cobb could be a gentleman. One day, to make a catch, he leaped into a roped-off area of bleacher fans in the Philadelphia outfield and accidentally crushed a spectator's straw hat. To hearty applause at the beginning of the next inning he presented the fan with five dollars to buy a new hat.

By the end of 1909 he had become the outstanding figure in professional baseball, leading the American League in batting (.377), as well as in hits, runs, stolen bases, and even in home runs (9).

The years just ahead, 1910 to 1917, were to become the greatest in his career, years marked by achievements that still live on in baseball history.

"Baseball," Ty Cobb once said, "is not unlike a war." To him, it was a game of matching trick against trick, and of making opponents tremble with fear before they could make him tremble. In such a game, declared Cobb, "the baserunner has the right of way and the man who blocks it does it at his own peril."

As a warrior in such a conflict, Cobb used many weapons. To get on base he usually would swing away. But he also slapped at balls, poked at them, bunted. While standing at the plate he sometimes said things to anger the pitcher, or even turned his back, paying no attention to what was being thrown. The result would often be a base on balls from a hurler upset by such antics. And once on base, Cobb became a ferocious runner.

Surprisingly, despite his high intelligence the Detroit star remained deeply superstitious. When things went well for him he insisted on wearing the same soiled uniform day after day. He would put on the same baseball sock first, eat the same food day after day, take the same streets to the ballpark. To him the idea of luck was crucial.

Altogether apart from good luck, Cobb's performance improved year after year. In 1911 he batted .420, making 248 hits and knocking in 144 runs—figures that would be career

Cobb won twelve American League batting championships, nine of them in a row. He compiled a lifetime batting average of .367, an achievement yet to be equaled. *Courtesy of National Baseball Library & Archive, Cooperstown, New York*

highs for him. In the same year he stole 83 bases. That figure, while below his highest mark of 96 in 1915, still stands far beyond the steals for entire teams in big league baseball today.

In the off-season Cobb busied himself with golf and hunting. He also became involved in automobile racing, once driving a car at the then spectacular speed of 105 miles per hour. The money from his rapidly growing salary went into cotton stocks, copper-mining ventures, and the growing industry of automobile construction. A natural saver, he was before long a man of considerable wealth.

To Cobb a career in baseball was "a wearing, a tearing life." But, as he put it, "the game is worth the candle."

Despite his success in sports and in business, as well as his supposed maturity in terms of years, Ty Cobb remained a person of fiery temper. Once a spectator in New York, sitting close to the Detroit dugout, repeatedly called him a "half nigger." The angry Southerner finally exploded, climbing into the seats and ferociously beating the fan, even though the man, as it turned out, had one hand missing and only three fingers on the other hand. For that act Cobb was suspended and fined by the American League's executive office.

On another occasion he argued with a black man working in a butcher shop. Drawing the pistol he often carried with him, Cobb struck the worker's head several times before fracturing his own thumb.

In 1918 Ty Cobb found himself in still another kind of conflict. He joined with most other Americans in supporting President Woodrow Wilson and the Congress in a declaration of war against Germany. During that baseball season he led the American League in batting for the eleventh time. Then, in October, he became a captain in the U.S. Army's Chemical Warfare Service.

Other famous athletes, including pitcher Christy Mathewson, joined the same military unit. The war was destined to end soon, in November 1918, but not before a serious accident nearly cost the two baseball stars their lives.

Training soldiers in the use of gas masks, they found themselves in a chamber without their masks on when, suddenly, gas was accidentally released. Mathewson, who inhaled far more of the fumes than Cobb, died seven years later of tuberculosis. Cobb believed that Mathewson's death resulted from the gas incident.

America's great victory on the battlefield did little to reduce Cobb's aggressive behavior on the ball field or outside. Following a 1919 game in St. Louis he kneed in the groin a fan who had been annoying him. Then he challenged every man in the surrounding crowd to fight. All of them refused.

It was during the 1919 season that Cobb failed to win the batting crown. Meanwhile, crowds of fans had begun to cheer wildly for another athlete, a New York Yankee who in the same year hit an astounding total of 54 home runs. His name was Babe Ruth.

Perhaps because of Ruth's growing fame, Cobb made a move on his thirty-fourth birthday, December 18, 1920—a decision he later regretted deeply. He agreed to become player-manager of the Detroit Tigers.

With the passage of time, Cobb's dislike for Babe Ruth turned to hatred. Clearly, Ruth's style of play—based on the hitting of home runs—challenged the reputation of Ty Cobb as the greatest player in the history of baseball. But to the fierce yet highly controlled Tiger star there also were important personal differences.

Whereas Cobb practiced great care in the foods he ate and in his use of alcohol, Ruth was exactly the opposite. The Yankee slugger ate enormous quantities of hamburgers and hot dogs even while games were being played. Unlike the disciplined Cobb, he would first appear at spring training camp looking fat and blubbery.

At night Ruth became drunk, spending his time with woman after woman in cities across the country. Still, his amazing success as a home run hitter soon made him the leading challenger to Cobb's reputation as the greatest player in baseball history.

Cobb made little effort to hide his dislike for the popular slugger. When Ruth passed the batting cage before a game Cobb would ask teammates if they suddenly "smelled" something. Making fun of Ruth's large nose and broad facial features, he spoke of him as a "nigger."

Before long, the two great stars of baseball became deep personal enemies.

As a manager Cobb acted in fierce competition with all the opposing teams—and also with umpires. While the Tigers batted he wildly paced the third-base coach's box, shouting encouragement to his players and exchanging sharp comments with fans.

Once, an umpire called him out in an attempt to steal home. Furious with the decision, Cobb challenged the umpire to fight it out in a locker room after the game. Another player later described the battle as the bloodiest he ever had seen.

Despite his terrible temper, Cobb spent hours as a teacher, carefully instructing such promising young Tiger hitters as Heinie Manush and the future batting champion Harry Heilmann. Less knowledgeable and less patient with his pitchers, he still worked hard to teach them what he could.

By 1924 Ty Cobb had become even wealthier through investment in the new soft drink Coca-Cola. His Detroit Tiger teammates respected greatly his accomplishments on the field. Fans across the nation knew that, as a manager as well as a player, he was intelligent, driven, and passionate in his style.

Yet, still, Cobb had not quite grown up. He encouraged his players to fight with their opponents. He spoke angrily to personal enemies, such as Babe Ruth, once actually going after the Yankee slugger on the playing field. He punched a black groundskeeper for refusing him the use of a stadium telephone. Despite his wealth he wrestled with a restaurant owner and then with a police officer about the bill charged him in a restaurant.

Late in his thirties, he remained in many ways a hot-tempered child—and always would be one.

Still, there occasionally was progress. As spectators at the 1924 World Series, Ty Cobb and Babe Ruth shook hands. They spoke to each other. And they began to build what eventually would become a real friendship.

At the end of the 1926 season Cobb resigned as manager of the sixth-place Detroit Tigers. Some of his players openly declared at the time that Cobb had been too tough with them, too demanding. He was, they said, so good a player himself that he could not understand why they were not. During the previous season eleven players actually had approached the owner of the Tiger baseball team asking to be traded. Cobb, they said, was the problem.

After his resignation, however, a more serious charge soon became public. Former Detroit Tiger pitcher Dutch Leonard formally charged that Ty Cobb and another great hitter and manager, Tris Speaker, once had set up the results of a game to win money on bets.

Cobb, competitive—and already rich—was furious. "Is there any decency left on earth?" he asked angrily. Even some of his former enemies declared that nobody with Cobb's competitive personality ever could have been involved in such a crooked scheme.

Following the 1919 "Black Sox Scandal," when several Chicago White Sox players admitted to throwing the World Series in exchange for money, Judge Kenesaw Mountain Landis had been appointed commissioner of baseball. In the Cobb-Speaker case, Landis finally declared the two men innocent.

"These players," he said in an official statement to newspapers, "have not been, nor are they now, found guilty of fixing a ball game. By no decent system of justice could such a finding be made."

Almost immediately after the verdict was announced, Connie Mack of the Philadelphia Athletics offered Cobb a contract making him, almost certainly, the highest-paid player in baseball.

Nearly forty years old and tired, Cobb felt obliged to return to baseball once again. Only in that way, he said, could he prove himself to the public.

Returning to play against the Detroit Tigers early in the season, he was presented with an automobile in admiration by

Cobb poses in his baseball uniform. *Courtesy of National Baseball Library & Archive, Cooperstown, New York*

his former Tiger fans. For those in the temporary outfield bleachers he signed hundreds of autographs. In the weeks that followed he again stole many bases, including several steals of home plate. He also managed to record his four thousandth major league hit—an achievement unequaled until more than sixty years later.

Playing in nearly all of his team's games and relieved of the pressures of managing, he finished the season with a splendid batting average of .357.

Still, Cobb often found himself exhausted during the long baseball season. He had assumed that the year would be his last as a professional player. By then his wife had given birth to five children. His personal fortune was considerable.

Yet when the next season began, Ty Cobb once again found himself standing at the plate. In June of that year he succeeded in stealing home plate for the thirty-fifth—and final—time in his awesome career. For the entire season he managed to bat a respectable .323.

The 1928 season, however, was to be Cobb's last. After more than three thousand games in the major leagues and a lifetime batting average of .367—still unequaled in baseball history—Ty Cobb, forty-one years old, finally retired.

But what of the future? A millionaire, he had no need to work in order to support himself and his family. What would he do with his time? Passionately loving the tension and excitement of the ball field, what now would become of him? How would he spend his time?

Cobb continued to invest in stocks and to become even wealthier. He and his wife traveled to other countries, both in Europe and in Asia, sometimes with their children.

In 1932 they bought a beautiful home near San Francisco—an enormous mansion with swimming pool, guesthouse, and servants' quarters. At least on the surface, everything in his life looked perfect, perhaps even ideal.

But really it was not. Most of the Cobb children described their father as a rigid disciplinarian, one who insisted on telling them exactly what to do. One son, Tyrus Raymond Cobb, Jr., came to hate the game of baseball. He lived a wild life as a student and an automobile driver, finally flunking out of Yale University.

Even more painful for the baseball superstar was word, in April 1931, that his wife, Charlie, had started the process of divorce from him. Somehow he managed to change her mind, at least for a while: sixteen more years. In 1947 the two finally parted, marking an end to nearly forty years of marriage.

Meanwhile, the glory of Ty Cobb's baseball career lived on, and even grew. In 1936 he had received the highest number of votes cast for admission to the newly organized Baseball Hall of Fame, with even Babe Ruth, his former rival, finishing behind him. The only other figures elected at the time were shortstop Honus Wagner and pitchers Christy Mathewson and Walter Johnson.

Even today those first five members of the Hall of Fame stand high in the total history of the game. Cobb, of course, realized the importance of his selection at the head of the list, declaring he was "overwhelmed" by it. Indeed he probably was more proud of that event than of any other in his baseball career, perhaps in his life.

Still, that life continued to pass rapidly on. In the 1940s Cobb learned of the deaths of close companions in the baseball world: Yankee first baseman Lou Gehrig, "Black Sox" slugger "Shoeless" Joe Jackson, and finally, Babe Ruth.

Soon afterward, two of Cobb's sons, Herschel and Ty, Jr., passed away. To Cobb's satisfaction, Ty, Jr., had managed to reverse his early undisciplined habits and become a doctor.

Meanwhile the baseball star had married again. His new wife, forty-four-year-old Frances Fairburn Cobb, like her famous sixty-two-year-old husband, liked to play golf, to hunt, and to travel. Early in their marriage she attended with Ty the formal opening of a hospital he had helped to finance in Georgia, dedicated to the memory of both his parents.

As he grew older, Cobb began to drink more and more heavily. He also insisted on keeping a notebook filled with references to people he hated, including his first wife, Baseball Commissioner Kenesaw Mountain Landis, and President Franklin Delano Roosevelt, who, according to Cobb, had ruined the Democratic party.

As the years went by, Cobb's anger, along with his feeling of unhappiness, increased. And so did his drinking.

Finally, in 1956, Frances Cobb divorced her husband.

From then on, he was alone—and lonely. Often he traveled from place to place across the country, sometimes appearing at old-timers baseball celebrations in major league stadiums, or in Cooperstown at the Baseball Hall of Fame. Although he received award after award, he still remained unhappy.

Physicians warned him that he had serious problems: diabetes, high blood pressure, a weak heart. Still, Cobb would travel frequently to Reno, Nevada, to gamble in casinos, to drink, to try to forget his personal problems. Usually he carried with him in a paper sack many thousands of dollars in negotiable securities—as well as a loaded Luger pistol.

Lonely, unhappy, and ever weaker physically, Cobb still managed to stay active. Once, he threw out the first ball in the spring opening of the newly formed Los Angeles Angels. But feeling ill, he left after the second inning.

To his elderly friend, comedian Joe E. Brown, Cobb sometimes admitted privately that he had made mistakes in his life. If he were to live it all over again, he said, he would be less aggressive. Maybe, then, he would have "had more friends."

Finally he was admitted to a hospital in Georgia. There, his former wife Charlie and his three remaining children came to visit him.

On Monday, July 17, 1961, Ty Cobb died at the age of seventy-four.

In the years following Cobb's death, black professional baseball players Maury Wills, Lou Brock, and Rickey Henderson all broke his single-season record of 96 stolen bases. Ironically, given Cobb's racial views, it was those black athletes who proved his point that there was more to baseball than the hitting of home runs.

Other athletes, too, would surpass some of Cobb's formidable records. In his very successful career Pete Rose, for example, managed to make more total hits.

Still, no player ever has matched Cobb's overall achievement. True there was great personal cost in what he accomplished—both to himself and to those on the diamond in whom he aroused hatred and fear.

Yet to people who knew him, he had qualities never to be

forgotten. Or as onetime New York Yankee manager and baseball star Casey Stengel put it, "It was like he was superhuman."

Looking back on his own life, a few months before he died, Ty Cobb thought especially about his father. "He never got to see me play," said Cobb. "But I knew he was watching me, and I never let him down."

GEORGE HERMAN ("BABE") RUTH

(1895–1948)

Courtesy of National Baseball Library & Archive, Cooperstown, New York

Babe Ruth! In the entire history of the United States few names have been so well known to so many people. To anger American soldiers during World War II their Japanese foes would often shout as loudly as possible, "To hell with Babe Ruth!" It was the insult they were convinced would hurt Americans the most.

Even today Ruth undoubtedly is better known than many of the nation's presidents. He is remembered as an extraordinary home run hitter and as the star of the New York Yankees in years when they dominated the world of baseball. People still talk of the time when, in a dramatic World Series game, Ruth supposedly pointed to the distant center field bleachers and then hit a pitch into the astonished crowd that was seated there.

Stories live on, too, about the tremendous number of hot dogs he would eat between innings of a game, and his willingness to be kind to kids, even visiting them in their hospital rooms when they were ill. Other stories tell of him as a wild drinker, a man who would stay up all night with women before going to the ballpark the next day.

His life has been the subject of numerous books. A movie made about him attracted huge audiences. At the Baseball Hall of Fame in Cooperstown, New York, crowds of visitors still are fascinated by his achievements on the field. Many people are also aware of events that marked his deeply troubled personal existence.

• • •

"Little George," as his parents called him, was born in Baltimore, Maryland, probably on February 6, 1895, but possibly on February 7, 1894; the exact date is uncertain. His father, "Big George," ran a saloon. His mother had lost several children at the time of their birth or in early infancy, and often was ill.

Even as a child the future baseball immortal lived a stormy life. He drank whiskey, chewed tobacco, frequently stole, threw apples at passing cars and trucks, and thought of the police as his enemies. In effect "Little George" tried to do exactly as he pleased. As he later remembered it, "I was a bad kid."

Thus, after several incidents of theft and truancy before he reached the age of eight, George's parents decided to withdraw him from public school. Instead they sent him to live at Saint Mary's Industrial School for Boys on the outskirts of Baltimore.

In the years that followed, young Ruth sometimes returned to live at home. But until he reached the age of twenty and signed a contract to play professional baseball, most of his time was spent behind the gates of Saint Mary's, under the strict guidance of Catholic Brothers in the Xaverian religious order.

One religious figure there, Brother Matthias, became Ruth's personal hero or, as he later put it, "the greatest man I've ever known . . . [and] the father I needed." Yet even with the kindness and attention given him by Brother Matthias, Ruth became known for his reckless temper and his willingness to break the rules of the school. Nevertheless Matthias always stood by him, later remembering how popular young George had always been with his classmates and how he sometimes would even take the blame—and the punishment—for acts that friends committed.

As Ruth passed into his teens he trained for a career in shirtmaking. But actually he spent more and more time at Saint Mary's playing baseball, again under the close discipline and teaching of Brother Matthias. Although a "lefty," George served as a catcher, sometimes forcing the usual left-handed catcher's mitt onto his right hand so he could throw more easily. From the beginning he showed enormous power with the bat, hitting at least one home run in most of the games he played.

One day in the spring of 1913, when Ruth was eighteen years old, a scout for the Baltimore Orioles, then the city's minor league team, came to watch him play. By then he had become a pitcher, and in that game pitched a 6–0 shutout, striking out twenty-two batters.

The following winter, before the Orioles were to leave for spring training, the same scout who had seen him in action, Jack Dunn, returned to Saint Mary's. He signed young Ruth to a contract paying one hundred dollars a month, six hundred dollars for the season. The Xaverian Brothers, by then totally responsible for him, agreed to the contract. With that act Ruth at last was on his own, altogether in command of his fate—something he long had desired. In later years he recalled the pleasure of telling his friends that he was going to play baseball for real money. Both then and afterward, money was, to him, less valuable in itself than as proof of his success in life.

When Ruth reported for spring training at the Orioles' camp in Fayetteville, North Carolina, he stood six feet two inches

tall and weighed a solid 180 pounds. In his first game of pre-
season play, his second time at bat, he hit a home run, the
longest drive ever recorded at that particular ballpark. His
pitching drew tremendous praise. Jack Dunn, the scout, soon
afterward described him as the most promising young
ballplayer he ever had seen—"a natural."

In fact, so great was Dunn's praise that people began
speaking of Ruth as "Dunn's baby," or more simply as "Babe."
Before long the name caught on and, from then on, he
became known as Babe Ruth.

The fatherly Dunn, however, could do little to shape
Ruth's personal habits. Crude and raw in his speech and man-
ners, "the Babe" was also an enormous eater, something that
caused much laughter among the older players. They teased
him, too, about his love for riding a borrowed bicycle at ter-
rific speeds. Once the regular season began Babe used his first
paycheck to buy a bicycle of his own.

From the very beginning, Ruth pitched well and hit well.
Thus, when the Orioles experienced serious financial difficulties in 1914 the owners had no problem in selling him for an
attractive sum to the Boston Red Sox, then one of the most
successful major league ball clubs. After only one season in the
minors he had made it to the big leagues.

His early experience with the Red Sox, however, produced only mixed results. As a pitcher Ruth sometimes was
hit hard. At the same time, his new teammates objected to his
insistence on taking batting practice with them, something
pitchers rarely did in those days. As a person, they considered him a "fresh kid." For whatever the reason, he had few
opportunities to play. By mid-August the Boston management decided to send him to Providence in the International

A portrait shot of a young Babe Ruth in his Red Sox days. *Courtesy of National Baseball Library & Archive, Cooperstown, New York*

League so he could spend more time in action on the mound.

Meanwhile he had come to know a pretty young waitress, sixteen-year-old Helen Woodford. Shortly after the season ended, Babe Ruth and Helen married. For that winter they lived in a small apartment above the saloon in Baltimore still owned by Ruth's father.

George, Sr., urged his son to stay on in Baltimore permanently and work in the saloon. But in February 1915 the Babe celebrated what he then thought was his twenty-first birthday (possibly only his twentieth). No longer could his father or the staff at Saint Mary's have control over his decisions. He knew for certain that when springtime came he would be reporting to the Florida training camp of the Boston Red Sox.

The 1915 season produced real satisfaction for young Ruth. In that year the Red Sox won the American League championship and then defeated the Philadelphia Phillies in the World Series. Babe pitched far less than he wanted to, but was beginning to be recognized for his talent at the plate as well as on the mound. With the share of money he received for Boston's victory in the Series (more than he had earned for the entire year) Ruth bought a new saloon for his father, spending the entire winter working for him as a bartender.

The next season became one of great success for the budding star. He won 23 games, a spectacular 9 of those victories as shutouts. Then, in the World Series, he pitched the entire contest in an exciting 2–1 fourteen-inning triumph of the Red Sox over the Brooklyn Dodgers. Some baseball historians consider that game one of the most dramatic postseason contests ever played. Boston went on once again to win the world championship easily.

In 1917 the Sox failed to repeat their triumph in the American League race, but Ruth still managed to win twenty-four games, six of them shutouts. Meanwhile, only three players in the league, including Ty Cobb, finished with a higher batting average than his .325. As a result, he won for the next year a salary increase of two thousand dollars, bringing him to seven thousand, then considered much more than merely a comfortable income; it was sensational. Yet, to Ruth, the money was understandable, since, as he later remembered it, "I was a great pitcher."

Perhaps because of his success Ruth turned to extremes in his personal life. Sometimes he would eat an entire pie for dessert, and his weight soon climbed above 215 pounds. Often he visited gambling casinos and racetracks, as well as spending evenings with women other than his wife.

The Red Sox management had begun to take his role as a hitter seriously. Thus, once the 1918 season began he frequently found himself playing the outfield between pitching assignments. In one series of four games Ruth hit four home runs, an astonishing feat for that time, since the baseballs then in use were dead balls—much less lively than those used today.

In some cases he absolutely refused to take the mound, claiming that his pitching arm or his wrist hurt. Disagreement over that issue, along with personal matters, grew increasingly heated until, finally, Ruth simply left the team, taking a job in a Baltimore shipyard. When at last the quarrel was settled he returned to competition, having agreed to play both in the outfield and on the mound. By the end of the summer he had registered 13 victories, winning 9 of his last 11 starts. He also managed to bat exactly .300 and to tie for the league leadership in home runs with 11.

As a pitcher in the World Series he defeated the Chicago Cubs 1–0 and 2–1. Such a performance was amazing. Before the Cubs finally managed to bring home a run against him he established a new record of 29 consecutive shutout innings in World Series competition, a success destined to stand in the record book until Whitey Ford of the Yankees broke it in 1961.

Following the end of World War I, American fans began to crowd major league baseball stadiums in even larger numbers for the 1919 season. And, by then, the star receiving the greatest attention was Babe Ruth. As a result, he bargained for—and won—a salary of ten thousand dollars a year, with only Ty Cobb receiving a larger amount.

Still, whatever money he earned, he spent—at least that much and often even more. He spent on cars, on clothing, on parties, on gambling, and on women, including his wife, Helen. *Fun* was truly what he wanted more than anything else, especially fun for *himself*.

Sometimes the time he spent at all-night parties led to bitter quarrels with his manager, Ed Barrow, since he remained awake for an entire night even when there was a game to be played the next day.

Yet, perhaps because of his natural talent, Ruth succeeded in hitting more and more home runs. During the 1919 season he slugged four homers with the bases loaded, a success that survived as a baseball record for forty years into the future. By the end of the year he had 29 home runs. In the history of the game nobody before had ever hit that many in a single season.

Overnight Babe Ruth became a national hero. Little could anyone imagine that in the next year, 1920, he would hit 54 home runs, a then unbelievable achievement, or that he was destined to lead the American League in home runs twelve times in his career. When finally he retired in 1934 the Babe had compiled a total of 714 home runs, along with 15 in World Series games, more than double the number of any other player active in his era.

Strangely, in the winter following Ruth's 1919 success with his then record total of 29 round trippers, he was traded away by the Boston Red Sox. That club's owner found himself faced with serious financial problems and, as a way out of his difficulties, sold Ruth to the New York Yankees for the princely sum of $125,000 in cash and a loan of $300,000.

Today, Red Sox fans who were not even alive at that time continue to criticize the deal, calling it the beginning of their team's bad luck. On the other hand, it was destined to mark a dramatic turning point in the success of the Yankees. It also was fated to transform the future of the sport of baseball in America.

During 1920, Ruth's first season as a New York Yankee, he hit .376, not enough to win the American League batting championship but a figure far beyond what today is registered by major league leaders. He also hit safely in 26 consecutive games, clubbed 9 triples and 36 doubles, and batted in 137 runs. Despite his weight, he stole 14 bases.

Most remarkably, however, Ruth slugged 54 home runs for the season. Closest to him in the American League was George Sisler, with 19 homers, while the National League leader recorded a total of only 15. Almost every team in both leagues registered a total number of home runs far below the 54 of Babe Ruth alone.

Wherever Ruth played, huge crowds jammed ballparks to see him. At the Polo Grounds, then the Yankees' home stadium, attendance soared to a new major league record of almost 1.3 million, close to four hundred thousand more than ever before in the club's history.

Following ball games, hundreds of fans mobbed to greet him. Autograph hunters begged for his signature. In New York the city's large Italian immigrant population took his nickname of "Babe" and spoke of him lovingly as "the Bambino" ("the baby").

Before long, players across the major leagues rushed to copy his style, eagerly trying for home runs, thus bringing them contempt from the older stars. Ty Cobb in particular still was committed to winning the usual low-score games by using the bunt, the stolen base, and the hit-and-run play.

But Babe Ruth had changed all of that, victorious not by intelligence, but by sheer power in his swing. To the vast majority of fans the home run had won out over the bunt as a source of excitement.

Ruth continued to stand out, too, in terms of his personal conduct. His roommate on road trips once remarked that he didn't really room with Babe since, as he put it, "I room with his suitcase."

Ruth often was welcomed at parties along with famous movie stars. He drove expensive cars at breakneck speeds. He bet vast amounts of money on horse races. He used profane, vulgar words, not only on the ball field but in other public settings, sometimes with women present. He drank vast quantities of alcohol, even though during the period of Prohibition, drinking was illegal. Still, despite all of his flaws, he had a personal charm that most people found almost irresistible.

For Ruth the 1921 baseball season proved enormously satisfying. He hit 59 home runs, batted .378, and with 204 bases on balls to his credit, managed to be on base more than half of the times he came to the plate. The Yankees, however, lost the World Series to the New York Giants, while Ruth, suffering from a badly injured elbow, was unable even to play in three games of the fall classic.

After his elbow healed he began to play in exhibition games, something that was then illegal for players on pennant-winning teams. When the commissioner of baseball, Judge Kenesaw Mountain Landis, ruled that Ruth no longer could participate in such games, the Yankee star became furious.

Always eager to challenge authority figures, whether they were schoolteachers, police officers, or the commissioner of baseball, he continued to play in the games. Landis finally imposed a fine of $3,362 each on Ruth and two Yankee teammates—their entire share in the recent World Series—and prohibited them from playing in the first six weeks of the 1922 season.

Few seasons were to prove so disappointing to "the Bambino" as 1922. When fans discovered that the Yankees were paying him the phenomenal amount of fifty-two thousand dollars, they greeted him on his eventual return to play with boos and hisses. Other great stars of the game, it was known, were being paid in the range of only four thousand to sixteen thousand dollars.

Expecting, as in the past, to be admired and cheered by spectators, Ruth began to lose his temper on the ball field. In one case he threw dust in the face of an umpire who called him out on a close play at second base after he had tried to stretch a single into a double. Then, when spectators shouted at him and called him profane names, he leaped into the stands and challenged them all to a fight. For that he was fined and suspended from play for several games by the president of the American League.

Later in the season Babe tried to fight with another umpire, and once again he was suspended without pay. By the end of the year he had been thrown out of competition a total of five times—still another Babe Ruth record that may never again be equaled.

Finally, in the 1922 World Series with the New York Giants, one of the Giants players called him a "nigger." After the game, in the Giants' clubhouse, it took crowds of players from both teams to prevent the furious Yankee slugger from attacking the name-caller. Eventually the Giants swept the World Series, defeating the Yankees four games to none.

The next season, 1923, proved very different. Ruth batted .393, his career high. He led the American League in home runs (41), as well as in runs batted in and runs scored. He even managed to record 17 stolen bases.

Also in 1923, Yankee Stadium opened. From the beginning it was known as "the house that Ruth built" because of profits from the enormous crowds that in past years had paid to see him play in the Polo Grounds. Fittingly, Ruth hit the first home run there. In the 1923 World Series he slugged three home runs to help the Yankees defeat their Manhattan rivals, the Giants, four games to two.

The next year, 1924, saw Ruth lead the American League not only in home runs, with 46, but also in batting, with an average of .378—the only time in his career that he captured that title. The Yankees, however, failed to win the pennant, finishing second to the Washington Senators. Ruth himself

Ruth at the plate in an exhibition game in Dunsmuir, California, on October 22, 1924. *Courtesy of National Baseball Library & Archive, Cooperstown, New York*

began drinking more heavily during that year, spending many nights out with women.

Not surprisingly, it was in 1925 that, following bitter quarrels, Babe and Helen Ruth finally separated. The Yankee great had meanwhile become serious about another woman, Claire Merritt Hodgson, a widow with one young daughter. But since both he and Helen were Catholics a divorce seemed unlikely.

Just before the 1925 baseball season began, Ruth experienced a severe stomach problem, one leading to major surgery. Because of its impact on his play it sometimes is described as "the stomachache heard round the world." By June, Babe was playing again but still remained weak, almost always looking exhausted.

To the disappointment of manager Miller Huggins, Ruth continued to eat heavily and to spend many nights drinking. As the star once put it himself, "I saw no reason why I could not play both day and night."

One day in late August, when Ruth appeared late for a game, Huggins finally lost all patience. He suspended Ruth from play and fined him five thousand dollars. At first the Babe was furious, protesting even to Baseball Commissioner Landis.

But so eager was he to play that eventually he apologized directly to Huggins. He decided to try even harder to be baseball's biggest attraction, but also to obey at least *some* of the rules. Remembering the incident with his manager many years later, he declared, "I acted like a spoiled child."

His determination paid off. Already thirty-two years old by the start of the 1926 season, Ruth was destined in his career to add more than 400 home runs to the 300 he thus far had hit. For the next six years his batting average would stand over the .350 mark and he would be the star in five World Series competitions. Already recognized in baseball history as a legend whose reputation would live on, he had no way of knowing that "the best was yet to come."

When spring training began in 1926 Ruth reported to camp in excellent physical condition, having exercised all winter and lost weight. He had begun to dress in less flashy clothing and to drive less showy cars. The parties he went to were calmer. His style of life was changing.

During the regular season he played in almost every game, hitting a total of 47 home runs, 28 circuit clouts more than his closest competitor! He batted .372, finishing second in the American League in that category, and he led the league in runs batted in with 155.

The 1926 World Series against the St. Louis Cardinals sometimes is seen as an embarrassment for Ruth. By the seventh and deciding game of the Series he already had slugged four home runs. Then, with two outs in the ninth inning of the final contest, he stood on first base with the potential tying run, the powerful Bob Meusel and Lou Gehrig coming to bat. Although speed was hardly Ruth's greatest strength, he tried to steal second base and was thrown out, giving victory to the Cardinals.

The Yankees of the next season, 1927, often are considered the finest team, and certainly one of the most interesting, in all of baseball history. In that year Lou Gehrig knocked in 175 runs and hit for a .373 average. He also won the Most Valuable Player Award. Ruth batted .356, driving in 164 runs.

But most dramatic of all was Babe's home run pace, gain-ing momentum as the season came into its final month and then its final days. Just one game was left to play when he succeeded in hitting his sixtieth home run. The record would last until 1961 when, with eight extra games added to the yearly big league schedule, Roger Maris clubbed 61. During the year of Ruth's great accomplishment no other team in the American League hit as many as the 60 home runs he personally slugged.

The 1927 Yankees finished an incredible nineteen games ahead of the second-place Philadelphia Athletics and then went on in the World Series to defeat the National League champion Pittsburgh Pirates in four consecutive games. In batting practice before the first game, with the Pirates watching them, Ruth and Gehrig pounded pitch after pitch into the right field seats, a feat their opponents found amazing.

The 1928 Yankees again captured the American League pennant, their third consecutive championship. In the World Series they triumphed over the St. Louis Cardinals, again sweeping the Series in four games. To the Yanks it was sweet revenge for the Cardinals' victory over them in 1926.

Babe Ruth himself pounded out ten hits in sixteen times at bat for an astonishing .625 average, one never again equaled in World Series history. In the final game he smashed three home runs off the Cardinal ace Grover Cleveland Alexander, ranked among baseball's greatest pitchers. Returning to New York from St. Louis by train, Ruth was greeted at every railroad station by crowds of wildly cheering fans.

In all, the year 1928, capped by Ruth's World Series performance, may well have marked a high point in his career.

· · ·

Ruth regularly received standing ovations. *New York Daily News*

What was Babe Ruth really like as a person? Some who knew him thought he was crude and vulgar in language and style, a man who cared little for the feelings of his wife, Helen, and thought only of himself. Yet even some of those who criticized the Babe admitted that he was the kind of person who could make life fun, a man who was enormously interesting and exciting.

At times Ruth would even forget the names of close companions and teammates, such as the pitcher Waite Hoyt, whom he once called "Walter." His enormous appetite continued to amaze everyone. At one breakfast he consumed an omelette containing eighteen eggs, along with ham, toast, and four cups of coffee. He also continued to be with many women, to drive cars far beyond the speed limits, to gamble, and to drink. More than one reporter described him as "an animal."

Ty Cobb, Ruth's longtime rival for the role of leading personality in baseball, showed special contempt for him. It was only many years after their retirement that the two came to express respect for each other. By and large Cobb tended to be bad-tempered on and off the field; the Babe had short bursts of temper that soon passed over.

Ruth made a special point of being nice to children. He would visit them in orphanages and hospitals. Later in life, when he was seriously ill himself, he expressed sympathy for youngsters who were suffering. His friends often remarked that Ruth seemed most at ease with children, feeling no need at all to prove himself to them, perhaps because in some ways he was almost "one of them." Or as he himself once put it, "I got as much of a kick out of them as they seemed to receive from their meetings with me."

Even after he was rich and famous he sometimes would

spend whole afternoons hitting fly balls to youngsters. He also visited prisons, where he sometimes showed inmates how to hit a baseball; he got along splendidly with the convicts.

Ruth's relationship with women was a very special matter for him. One night in July 1929, his wife, Helen, died in a fire. Although the couple had quarreled and had been living apart for more than three years, Babe was deeply moved by the tragedy. Both when he heard the news and at the funeral, he openly cried.

Only a few months later, however, he married Claire Merritt Hodgson, his close companion since the breakup with Helen. He cared deeply for Claire and her young daughter. He also found in them the kind of family situation he had missed as a child, when he had been sent early in life into the crowded, disciplined setting of Saint Mary's.

When they married, Ruth was thirty-five, Claire almost twenty-nine. In some ways she was destined to become to him a substitute for the mother he never really had. Indeed he sometimes even called her "Mom." Like a mother she corrected him, kept after him, even nagged him. But he always could be certain that she loved him.

Baseball fans loved him, too, turning out in large numbers to watch him play. In 1930 he signed a two-year contract with the Yankees for the then astonishing figure of eighty thousand dollars a year—far more than any other player had ever received. In 1932, when other players were taking deep cuts in pay because of the Great Depression, he was reduced only to seventy-five thousand dollars a year, the same salary as the president of the United States. Still, despite his phenomenal rewards, Ruth brought in to the Yankees far more money than he was paid.

• • •

In the 1932 World Series against the Chicago Cubs Ruth performed one of the truly memorable acts in baseball history:
pointing to the fence and then hitting a home run. In the first
inning at Wrigley Field, following two Yankee wins in New
York, Chicago players and their fans had openly razzed him,
yelling at him and calling out boos. Some fans even had
thrown lemons at him from the stands.

In the fifth inning Ruth responded dramatically by waving his arm outward to center field. After a first called strike
he raised a single finger. Following a second called strike he
raised two fingers.

Then, on the next pitch he slugged a line drive into the
center field bleachers, longer than any home run ever hit
before at that stadium. With all eyes of the silent crowd riv-
eted on him he circled the bases, laughing and shouting at the
Cub players. It was, as he later remembered it, "the funniest,
proudest moment I . . . ever had in baseball."

Lou Gehrig, the very next batter, followed with yet
another home run, and eventually enjoyed a more productive
Series than Ruth. But the incident of the precalled World
Series home run stands out even now as one of the truly
remarkable events in the Babe's illustrious career.

The years that followed were destined to prove less glorious
for Ruth. Because of hard times brought on by the Great
Depression, the Yankees cut his salary for 1933 from seventy-
five thousand dollars to fifty-two thousand. He still ranked by
far as the highest-paid player in the game, and to most Americans of that troubled era, he was a man of fantastic wealth.

Thanks to his wife, Babe actually began to save some of the money he earned.

Some baseball historians have been critical of Ruth's 1933 performance. Yet he managed to bat .301 and to hit 34 home runs. Furthermore, in the first All-Star Game ever played, held in July of 1933 at Chicago's Comiskey Park, it was Babe Ruth who slugged the very first home run of that classic event, as well as excelling in the field.

In the final game of the 1933 season, Ruth took the mound as a pitcher once again; the advance notice of that activity had drawn a large crowd to Yankee Stadium. To his satisfaction he defeated the team he formerly had pitched for, the Boston Red Sox, 6–5. When he left the stadium an hour afterward, some five thousand fans still were waiting to cheer him. Unable to raise his tired pitching arm to thank them, he instead used his right hand to graciously tip his cap.

Many of Babe's friends assumed that he would retire at the end of the 1933 season. Instead he decided to play a little longer, hoping to be appointed manager of a major league squad, possibly even the Yankees. But, for Ruth, 1934 proved disappointing: a .288 batting average and 22 home runs. Nevertheless, huge crowds still packed stadiums to watch him perform.

In the off-season a team of outstanding American players from both major leagues visited Japan, many of the stars accompanied by their wives. Possibly for publicity purposes, Babe Ruth was named as the team's field manager. During the seventeen games in Japan, Ruth played every inning and slugged 13 home runs to tremendous applause from audiences of over eighty thousand.

The Americans also played in China and the Philippine Islands, after which Ruth and his wife toured Europe. His only disappointment came in Paris, where scarcely anyone had ever heard of him. Speaking later of the Parisian experience he declared, "Nobody gave a damn."

On his return to America Ruth was approached by Emil Fuchs, owner of the National League's Boston Braves, with the prior approval of the Yankee management. The Braves' offer looked good to him: a salary of twenty-five thousand dollars plus a share in the club's profits, along with the title of vice-president and assistant manager of the team. Although not in writing, there at least was a hint that he might become the team's manager in 1936. Reluctant to leave the Yankees, he hoped above all to become a manager. So he signed the contract.

The 1935 season proved a disaster for him. Even after spring training in Florida he still weighed close to 250 pounds and moved far more slowly than in the past. He also continued to drink heavily. Meanwhile, Fuchs insisted that he invest money in the ball club.

Ruth grew increasingly unhappy, knowing that he was fat and old. Nevertheless, he still had natural ability. In a game played in Pittsburgh he hit three homers, one of them clearing the roof of Forbes Field, something that never before had been done.

That home run was his 714th in regular season play—and the last one he would ever hit.

At the end of May he hurt his knee trying to catch a fly ball. Unable to play, Ruth hoped to visit the famous new ocean liner *Normandie* when it docked in New York harbor. But Fuchs insisted that he stay on with the ball club. In response Babe announced that he was quitting the Braves altogether, not just as a player but as vice-president and assistant manager. Fuchs gave him an unconditional release, angrily labeling him a "poor sport."

Before that year Babe Ruth had played in professional baseball for twenty-one spectacular seasons. Although he clearly announced after leaving the Braves that he someday hoped to return to the major leagues as a manager, no offers came his way. Drinking was a major part of his problem. Most owners, too, thought little of his intelligence and maturity. Jacob Ruppert of the Yankees once declared that Ruth had "the mentality of a boy of fifteen."

Ruth had a large income from lifetime investments, so he had few worries about money. With free time at his command he became a wildly enthusiastic golfer. He swam, often racing people across pools. He was paid for speaking at banquets, and for appearing at boxing matches and professional golf tournaments. Quite often, however, he simply drank. Baseball to him had been a game played less for money than for sheer joy, and now that joy was gone.

In 1936 Ruth became one of the five players first elected to membership in the newly created Baseball Hall of Fame at Cooperstown, New York, the others being Ty Cobb, Honus Wagner, Christy Mathewson, and Walter Johnson. To the American nation, Ruth still was a hero of the first order.

In 1938 the Brooklyn Dodgers hired him as a coach, wanting no more than his presence on the field as a way of attracting fans to the ballpark. As the Dodger management had hoped, large crowds began to fill the stadium just to see him. Unlike most other players, Ruth always would remain after a game to sign autographs for the youngsters who gathered in large crowds to greet him.

Almost certainly Babe hoped to become manager of the ball club in 1939. But when it became known soon after the summer ended that the feisty Leo Durocher had been selected instead to head the Dodgers, Ruth announced his retirement. During the season he and Durocher, enemies from many years earlier, had engaged in a vicious fistfight.

On first learning of the appointment of "Leo the Lip" as manager, Ruth was reduced to tears. By then it had become clear to him that major league club owners had virtually no confidence in his ability to manage a team.

Before the 1939 season began, Ruth cried, too, when he visited Jacob Ruppert, the former Yankee owner, who then was dying in a hospital. That July, in a ceremony held at Yankee Stadium, he hugged his former teammate and friend, Lou Gehrig, who also was on the brink of death. Two years later, in 1941, in a movie about Gehrig called *Pride of the Yankees,* Ruth played himself. During World War II, the Babe did much to raise money for such charities as the Red Cross.

There was no doubt, however, that he was aging quickly. Late in 1946 doctors removed a cancerous growth from his throat, leaving him exhausted and able to speak only faintly. To many of his friends who knew him well it was clear that his condition was serious.

To honor him while he still was alive, the new commissioner of baseball, A. B. ("Happy") Chandler, declared April 27, 1947, "Babe Ruth Day" in every major league ballpark. Ruth himself appeared before a crowd of more than sixty thousand fans at Yankee Stadium.

After apologizing for the sound of his voice, he spoke

briefly, declaring to his fans, "The only real game in the world, I think, is baseball."

Ruth's condition grew worse, but on June 13, 1948, he appeared once again at the Stadium. Leaning on a bat to support himself, he told the crowd how proud he was to have hit the very first home run hit there.

The applause for him was tremendous.

By July he once again was back in the hospital. There he received more than fifty thousand letters, postcards, and telegrams, including a letter from the president of the United States, Harry S. Truman. Day by day Ruth's condition grew worse. He lost more and more weight and became almost too weak to talk.

On August 16, 1948, at the age of fifty-three, George Herman ("Babe") Ruth died.

The flag at the Baseball Hall of Fame in Cooperstown, New York, was lowered to half-mast. In a special funeral ceremony at Yankee Stadium perhaps as many as two hundred thousand people came to see his body. A major portion of his estate went to the Babe Ruth Foundation, dedicated to helping underprivileged children. For years afterward, his wife, Claire, appeared at ceremonies in his honor.

Even today, so long after Ruth's death, he still is remembered. For many fans around the world, to speak of baseball is to speak of Babe Ruth. He may well have been the most exciting, the most naturally gifted player the sport has known. By his incredible talent as a home run hitter he produced dramatic changes. Baseball became more open, a matter of fun and joy. To him, playing at it was always less a matter of work than of pleasure.

Today many of the remarkable records Babe Ruth established still survive, while the memory of his life lives on. In that sense his reputation for success appears in very real harmony with other great personalities of the nation's history. And now, as a player who shaped the game, he clearly shares the stage with those in the past who have helped to mold the American dream.

JOHN ROOSEVELT ("JACKIE") ROBINSON
(1919–1972)

National Baseball Library & Archive, Cooperstown, New York

Who was Jackie Robinson, and what did he accomplish that merits his placement alongside Ty Cobb and Babe Ruth as one of three men who shaped the game of baseball?

Undoubtedly Robinson was a great ballplayer. He was the National League's Rookie of the Year in 1947 and its Most Valuable Player in 1949. He won election in 1962 to the Baseball Hall of Fame, the first African American (or "Negro" as blacks were called in those days) ever chosen for that honor.

Today there are public schools named for him. He often is discussed in history textbooks used in the nation's schools. A picture of Jackie Robinson once appeared on a U.S. postage stamp. But perhaps the most lasting result of Robinson's life was to open the doors of professional baseball to black players.

After that happened, still other opportunities arose for blacks. If they could play professional baseball together with whites, should they not also be entitled to equal rights in the nation's armed forces, in schoolrooms, in neighborhood housing, and in jobs? Should they not play a larger part in government? Once Jackie Robinson succeeded as a major league player many of the other great barriers to the participation of blacks in American life quickly crumbled.

Always a fighter, Robinson became a hero for the nation's black people. He also proved to those of every race that ability, combined with hard work, high hopes, and dogged determination, could lead to triumph. His life story shows that what seem to be impossible dreams really can come true.

Jackie Robinson was born in Cairo, Georgia, on January 31, 1919, the fifth child of a sharecropper farmer, Jerry, and a mother, Mollie, whose own father had been a slave. Six months after Jackie's birth his father deserted the family, leaving for Florida with another man's wife.

Because one of Mollie's own brothers had moved to California and described it as "heavenly," she soon decided to follow him there. Settling in Pasadena, Mollie and all five of her children at first slept in one room of a tattered old slum building. Soon, however, she found work as a maid and moved the family to an otherwise all-white district of the city.

From the very beginning the Robinsons encountered prejudice in their new neighborhood. Jackie himself always remembered an incident that took place when he was eight years old. A white girl living in a house near his shouted at him, "Nigger! Nigger! Nigger!"

Robinson responded quickly, declaring that she was "nothing but a cracker" (a lower-class white person).

To that, the girl chanted:

"Soda cracker's good to eat;
Nigger's only good to beat."

In the years that followed, Jackie met with much more prejudice. Partly in response to it and partly because of poverty, he found himself involved in a street gang of young people (the Pepper Street gang), a childhood experience not unlike that of Babe Ruth. Robinson and the other boys would gather golf balls on a white country club course and then cash them in for money. They would throw dirt at passing automobiles. Sometimes they would steal.

Since neighborhood swimming pools usually were closed to blacks, Jackie and the others in his gang often did their own swimming in the Pasadena city reservoir. One day a sheriff and several deputies came by and found them at play. "Looka here!" shouted the sheriff. "Niggers swimming in my drinking water!"

Later, in the crowded police station, the sheriff gave the boys pieces of watermelon and then, waving his pistol, threatened that he had better not see them again.

Two neighbors, one of them a minister, played an important part in preventing young Jackie Robinson from becoming a delinquent. They convinced him that it didn't show real courage to be part of a gang, and that by just going along with the crowd he could hurt his mother, as well as his own future.

But probably it was success in sports that turned Jackie around. So remarkable was his ability that classmates in his elementary school sometimes even shared their lunches with him if he agreed to play on their teams.

By the time he finished high school Robinson had become known as a truly outstanding athlete, a star in football, basketball, track, and baseball. Next, at Pasadena Junior College, he broke several existing records in track while starring in the other sports as well. His performance on the football field was so exemplary that many colleges across the country offered him athletic scholarships. In order to stay close to his family, however, Jackie decided to attend the University of California at Los Angeles (UCLA).

Sadly, soon after he made that decision his older brother and close personal companion, Frank, was killed in a bicycle accident. It was a loss he never could forget.

For Jackie Robinson, attending UCLA became an experience filled with academic success and with high praise for his athletic achievements. He also met a girl, Rachel ("Rae") Isum. At first she considered him a cocky and arrogant "jock" athlete, but before long she grew to admire Jackie for his high grades in the classroom far more than his performance in sports.

Rachel's preference probably was the exception, since by that time, Jackie was being described by some observers as the greatest all-around athlete ever to play on the Pacific Coast. Never before had anybody succeeded so highly in so many different kinds of games. A few writers went so far as to call him "the greatest colored athlete of all time," even including the then world heavyweight boxing champion, Joe Louis.

Although Rae objected to it, Robinson left UCLA in his senior year to play for the Honolulu Bears, a professional football team in Hawaii. But when the season ended, he found himself short of money, and worked as a day laborer for a company building ammunition shelters near Pearl Harbor. That kind of effort, he soon decided, led absolutely nowhere. On December 5, 1941, he left on a ship headed for California, planning to work with young people in danger of falling victim to the kinds of problems with crime he once had experienced himself.

Two days after he left, on December 7, Japanese planes launched a surprise attack on Pearl Harbor, plunging the United States into World War II.

• • •

Because of a past injury in football Jackie Robinson was taken into the army on only a "limited service" basis. With the help of boxer Joe Louis, he and several other blacks were admitted to Officers Candidate School (OCS). On receiving his commission as an army lieutenant Robinson celebrated by purchasing an engagement ring for Rae.

As an officer Robinson soon came to see that black soldiers were not treated as well as whites. At the post exchange, for example, blacks were seated separately from whites, and made to stand in long lines even for candy bars and soft drinks. Robinson protested, but got nowhere. Soon afterward, because he was black he was denied the right to play on his camp's baseball team.

Still later, while riding a town bus in Texas, he was told to go to the very back of the bus, even though there were empty seats in the "white" section. Such segregation of blacks then was a common Southern practice. Robinson, however, refused to leave his seat. For that act of civil disobedience serious charges were brought against him by military authorities, in support of the local police.

He was found not guilty, but the experience proved important to Robinson. It convinced him that even in government service—the U.S. Army—blacks did not have the same rights as whites. Angry at what had happened, he requested a medical discharge from the service. Possibly because the army wanted to get rid of such a "troublemaker," the request was granted.

Robinson returned immediately to Los Angeles. There he first contacted Rachel Isum. Then, in April 1945, he signed a contract to play professional baseball with the Kansas City Monarchs, a team in the Negro American League. Those two factors—his love for Rachel and his involvement with baseball—were destined to shape the remainder of his life.

Although many black soldiers then were giving their lives in the bloody struggle against the dictatorships of Germany, Italy, and Japan, black baseball players still were not permitted to play in the major leagues. Perhaps because of the war, cries began to be heard to change that situation. On the cover of one pamphlet issued by a New York City councilman there appeared the picture of a black soldier, dead on the battlefield. Next to him was the picture of a black baseball player. The caption declared, "Good enough to die for his country, but not good enough for organized baseball."

Branch Rickey, general manager of the Brooklyn Dodgers, was determined to change such an unfair situation. Quietly, secretly, he began working to find a black with enough talent to succeed on the baseball diamond, but also with the character and personality to be accepted by the public when he wasn't in action on the field. Those qualities, he believed, were essential to success in permanently breaking the racial barrier. Rickey considered several players, including such eventual stars as catcher Roy Campanella and pitcher Don Newcombe. But his choice was Jackie Robinson.

Rickey personally visited UCLA, as well as Robinson's high school and junior college. He learned that Jackie neither drank nor smoked, had made good grades academically, had always dated well-mannered girls, and was a fierce competitor on the field with "lots of guts." To the Dodger administrator,

Robinson appeared to be just the right choice for so daring an experiment.

Robinson first met with Clyde Sukeforth, an aide to Branch Rickey, before appearing in Brooklyn on August 28, 1945, for an interview with Rickey himself. The two men spoke for three hours in a session that would change the history of baseball in America.

Rickey dramatically described—and acted out—what almost certainly would happen when Robinson began playing against whites. They would call him names; they would spike him; they would throw pitches at his head. Sometimes he wouldn't be able to eat in the same restaurants as his teammates or to stay at the same hotels. Even umpires would give him a hard time. Fans would boo him.

Most important of all, declared Rickey, in the beginning it would be impossible to fight back. Instead, he would have to "turn the other cheek" and simply play the game of baseball. "Resist not evil," said Rickey, quoting Jesus in the Bible. "Whosoever shall smite thee on thy right cheek turn to him the other also. . . ."

Robinson understood completely what the strong-willed baseball official was proposing to him. And although he knew it would be difficult, he accepted the challenge. That very same day he signed a contract with the Brooklyn Dodgers, agreeing to play his first season in the minor leagues, with the Montreal Royals. His salary was to be $600 a month, along with a bonus of $3,500 for signing.

Like a hurricane the story of Jackie Robinson's signing hit the newspapers, wire services, and radio networks. Reporters swarmed to interview him. Famous baseball greats, including

Rogers Hornsby and Bob Feller, declared that the experiment was bound to fail. White people on the streets of big cities and small towns across the country told jokes about the "nigger" player.

One person, however, who proudly cheered the Robinson contract was Rachel Isum. On February 10, 1946, she and Jackie were married. Aware that a stormy future almost certainly lay ahead of them, Rachel still felt strongly that she wanted to face it at Jackie's side.

For the newly married couple, Jackie and Rachel Robinson, the trip to spring training in Daytona Beach, Florida, proved to be a nightmare. At the airport in New Orleans there was no place for blacks to rest, no place for them to eat. In one restaurant the Robinsons were told they could buy food but would have to take it outside to eat. Shortly after that, whites were given the Robinsons' seats on a flight leaving for Pensacola, Florida. In Florida itself they would find signs on separate rest rooms: FOR COLORED WOMEN and FOR WHITE LADIES. Water fountains often were labeled FOR WHITES ONLY.

After finally reaching Daytona Beach the Robinsons were introduced to the Montreal Royals' manager, Clay Hopper, then active not only as a figure in professional baseball but as owner of a cotton plantation in Mississippi. Although Jackie could not know it, Hopper had strongly urged Branch Rickey not to add a black man to the Montreal roster and at first behaved with formal coolness to the newcomer. While watching Robinson during one game he turned to Rickey and asked him, "Mr. Rickey, do you really think a nigger's a human being?" The Dodger executive, as he later described the scene, simply refused to answer.

The regular 1946 baseball season began in Jersey City, New Jersey. In his second time at bat, with two runners on base, Robinson slugged a drive over the left field wall for a home run. Years later he still remembered how excited and happy a single swing of the bat had made him.

In his next time at bat he laid down a bunt for a single, stole second, and made his way to third on a groundout. When he pretended to start out on a steal of home plate the pitcher committed a balk and Jackie was allowed to score. The crowd roared its approval. Following the end of that game and the next two games of the series, hundreds of fans rushed onto the field to touch him, knowing that baseball history was being made.

But farther south, in Baltimore, Maryland, it was a different story. Fans yelled out curses about Robinson's skin color, his family, his supposed body odor. They booed him. Still, with many blacks seated in the stands, there were no actual attempts at violence.

Back in the Montreal Royals' home stadium, spectators cheered him wildly. Canadian sportswriters soon began comparing his bunting and stealing skills to those of Ty Cobb.

By the end of the season, despite all the tension surrounding his daily performance, Robinson managed to lead the league in batting and generally was recognized as its best-fielding second baseman. In his final appearance of the year in Baltimore he succeeded in stealing home plate. The once hostile, surly crowd there applauded loudly.

When he set out for spring training in 1947 Jackie understood that making the jump to the major leagues—to Branch Rickey's Brooklyn Dodgers—would not be easy. Pee Wee

Reese, the Dodgers' shortstop, was an all-star player, as was their second baseman, Eddie Stanky. Rickey proposed a solution: Jackie should play first base, something that, even as a child, he almost never had done. Initially uncertain, Robinson finally agreed to try. Rickey reminded him, too, that the real secret to his making the Dodger squad would be his style—bunting, stealing bases, playing aggressively.

Even before the team met for spring training Rickey learned that some of the Dodgers planned to circulate a petition declaring that they would not play on a team with a black. Included among the signers of the petition were such stars as pitcher Hugh Casey, from Georgia, outfielder Dixie Walker, from Alabama, and two Northerners, Cookie Lavagetto and Carl Furillo.

Rickey dealt with the protestors individually, and in each case firmly. Then, at the end of spring training, he issued an announcement to the press: The Dodgers officially had purchased from Montreal the contract of Jack Roosevelt Robinson. He would become part of the major league team immediately.

Once the actual season began Jackie found himself the target of sometimes vicious verbal attacks by members of opposing ball clubs. Ben Chapman, an Alabama native and manager of the Philadelphia Phillies, was particularly harsh, leading his players in calling Robinson "nigger" and shouting at him to go back to the cotton fields where he belonged.

Robinson's supporters, such as Eddie Stanky, accused the Phillies of attacking somebody who couldn't answer back. Even Dixie Walker surprisingly came to Jackie's defense against the Phillies' abuse.

Finally, the commissioner of baseball, A. B. ("Happy") Chandler, demanded that the bench jockeying be toned down. At the urging of Rickey, Chapman agreed to pose for a picture with Robinson, but he would do so only with the two of them holding on to a bat rather than shaking hands. Reluctantly, Jackie agreed. It was an incident he would never forget—and Chapman was a man he would never forgive.

A potentially far more serious situation loomed in early May, just before the Dodgers were to play their first game of the season in St. Louis. *New York Herald Tribune* writer Stanley Woodward learned that several St. Louis Cardinals players were planning a strike if Robinson's name actually appeared in the lineup. When Woodward informed Ford Frick, the president of the National League, of the Cardinals' intention, Frick exploded.

He warned the Cardinals:

If you do this you will be suspended from the league. You will find that the friends you think you have in the press box will not support you, that you will become outcasts. I do not care if half the league strikes. Those who do it will encounter quick retribution. They will be suspended, and I don't care if it wrecks the National League for five years. This is the United States of America, and one citizen has as much right to play as another.

The National League will go down the line with Robinson whatever the consequence. You will find if you go through with your intention that you have been guilty of complete madness.

There was no player strike in St. Louis.

The trouble for Jackie Robinson, however, did not stop. Virtually every day he received letters threatening to kill him, to hurt his wife, to kidnap his son, Jackie, Jr. To avoid personal conflict with teammates Robinson still made it a point to stay out of their poker games, reading a book instead.

After he finally did begin to play cards, Southerner Hugh Casey once declared, while drunk, that when he had bad luck at poker he usually tried to turn things around by rubbing the skin of a black woman. Furious, Robinson still managed to control his temper, instead stating quietly, "Deal, man, deal."

On the ball field, too, he controlled himself, not even hitting back when players on other teams intentionally spiked him.

By the end of the 1947 baseball season Robinson could look back with pride on his accomplishments. He had played in 150 of the 154 games, had batted a respectable .297, and had led the Dodgers in stolen bases.

To his great satisfaction he was chosen as the National League's Rookie of the Year. Even Dixie Walker, who had opposed Jackie's coming to the team, warmly praised his performance. Before the beginning of a "Jackie Robinson Day" held at Ebbets Field near the end of the season, Walker stood at home plate to give the black star his special congratulations.

Meanwhile, Rachel Robinson sat in the stands that day with tears in her eyes. Her husband had become by then perhaps the most widely known black man in the world.

At the beginning of the 1947 World Series, as Jackie remembered it: "I experienced a completely new emotion when the National Anthem was played. This time, I thought, it is being played for me, as much as for anyone else. This is organized major league baseball, and I am standing here with all the others; and everything that takes place includes me."

The year 1948 was far less eventful for Jackie Robinson, but one of solid performance on the diamond. He batted .296 and led the league's second basemen in fielding percentage. Then, just prior to the 1949 season, Branch Rickey informed him that, following three years of high courage and restraint, he at last was free, if he wished, to fight back. No longer was it necessary for him to "turn the other cheek."

By the time of the All-Star break at midseason Robinson led the league in batting, stolen bases, hits, and runs-batted-in. He polled 1,891,212 ballots for membership on the National League All-Star team, the highest vote total in the league. Never before had a black ballplayer taken the field in the classic All-Star contest. Once again, it was Jackie Robinson who led the way.

As time went by it became ever more clear that Robinson's role in American life went beyond affairs of the diamond. During the summer of 1949 he was asked to testify in Congress before the House Un-American Activities Committee, then looking into singer Paul Robeson's prediction that blacks would not fight if ever the United States found itself at war with the Communist-dominated Soviet Union. Jackie remembered that, while in the army, he had been court-martialed for speaking out firmly about the military's treatment of blacks. Still, he felt deeply that Robeson had been mistaken. Branch Rickey urged Jackie to testify.

And he did, declaring with strong conviction that blacks understood their responsibility to stand by their country and

Halfway through the 1949 season, Robinson led the league in batting, stolen bases, hits, and runs batted in. *National Baseball Library & Archive, Cooperstown, New York*

that he felt certain they would do so in time of trouble. Black Americans, he said, didn't need Communist assistance to gain their proper rights. "We can win our fight without the Communists and we don't want their help."

That very evening, following his congressional testimony, Jackie was the Dodger star in a game at Ebbets Field against the Chicago Cubs. For him it was typical of the 1949 season. He led the National League in batting that year with an average of .342, as well as in stolen bases with 37. Not surprisingly, he was presented with the league's Most Valuable Player Award.

Even when the Dodgers were playing on the road, huge crowds filled stadiums to see Robinson in action. Following the games, he would be surrounded by swarms of autograph seekers.

Increasingly, sportswriters began to compare Robinson to Ty Cobb. They wrote of Jackie's speed. Actually it was Robinson's technique of upsetting pitchers, much like that of Cobb, that made him so exciting a base runner. Once he reached base the entire opposing team, not just the pitcher, would become absorbed in what he might do next.

Yet, like Babe Ruth, when the need arose Robinson also could hit for distance. During the 1951 season the New York Giants had managed to gain a tie with the Dodgers for first place in the pennant race and then, by defeating the Boston Braves on the last day, had taken the lead. Meanwhile, Brooklyn was locked in a fourteen inning tie with the Philadelphia Phillies.

It was then that Jackie Robinson stepped to the plate against one of the greatest pitchers in baseball history, Robin Roberts. Although exhausted and ill, Robinson slammed a

Roberts pitch into the seats for a home run, throwing the entire pennant race into a postseason playoff with the Giants.

As time passed, Jackie's achievements were recognized as solid and substantial. He batted .328 in 1950 and .338 in 1951. In 1951 he set a new fielding record for second basemen with a percentage of .992. Clearly, he had become one of the stars of the game.

Yet Robinson did not succeed in baseball on his own. One of his strongest supporters was Pee Wee Reese, the Dodger shortstop. Although from Kentucky, a state where blacks were segregated from whites in schools, transportation facilities, restaurants, and washrooms, Reese believed in fairness for all. He was the one who first invited Jackie to join in poker games, along with such Dodger players as Preacher Roe and Billy Cox. He did the same in golf, so that Robinson eventually played on the course with almost all of his teammates.

Perhaps the most famous example of friendship between the two came in a ball game with the Boston Braves, with Reese at shortstop and Robinson at second base. Players on the Boston bench jeered loudly at Reese, a Southerner, for playing alongside a black. At first Reese ignored the catcalls, rubbing his glove and looking toward home plate.

Then, as the tirade continued, he walked to Jackie Robinson's side and put his arm around his teammate's shoulder, speaking to him as a friend. As he did so, the Braves dugout fell silent. Reese had shown that he was there to play baseball, not to get involved in childlike teasing.

The scene marked a turning point in the way many National League ball clubs treated Robinson. Pee Wee Reese was the player most responsible for the change.

Reese admired Robinson greatly and wondered whether

he himself would have had the courage to stand up to the taunting of opposing teams and of spectators. Robinson, he said, was "my kind of man." It was a very few players like Pee Wee Reese who helped Robinson become part of the game, so that what eventually would matter most was not the color of his skin but how he performed on the field.

Even after his triumph as the first black man to succeed in major league baseball, Jackie Robinson remained a person of controversy. Some fans and reporters considered him too aggressive. Others spoke of him as a "loud mouth," or "too big for his britches." As he himself admitted, he remained at least as much concerned about matters of race and politics as about his batting average or his success on the base paths.

Black players who followed him to success, such as the Dodger catcher Roy Campanella, tried to avoid controversy, especially as related to their skin color. To Robinson, principles of race were matters worth fighting for.

After Walter Alston became manager of the Dodgers and Walter O'Malley replaced Branch Rickey as the team's chief executive officer, Jackie became increasingly unhappy. He felt that Alston knew far less about the sport than Chuck Dressen, the former manager, and also lacked Dressen's tough-minded, competitive spirit. O'Malley, meanwhile, refused even to accept Jackie's anger at still being forced to stay in the rundown "black only" hotels like those he had used on first joining the team in 1947.

Along with the personal problems he faced with Alston and O'Malley, Robinson found the 1955 season difficult on the field. He stole fewer bases, hit for a lower average, made more errors. At the age of thirty-six he found himself slowing

down. Still, he starred for the Dodgers in the 1955 World
Series, playing a major role in their dramatic victory over the
New York Yankees. Some of the Dodgers believed that it was
his daring steal of home plate in the first game that really
turned the tide.

By the end of the 1956 season, however, Jackie concluded
that his time for retirement from baseball had arrived. During
the winter he confidentially accepted a position with the
Chock Full o'Nuts restaurant chain while also agreeing, for
fifty thousand dollars, to have *Look* magazine do a summary
article on his career.

But before the official announcement of his decision to
retire or the publication of the article in *Look,* Walter O'Malley
traded Robinson to the New York Giants.

For Jackie it was an awkward situation, and for a time he
even considered playing for one more year. Instead, to the
anger of O'Malley, Robinson formally announced his retirement. The sport had done much for him, but he also had
done much for baseball—and for the status of blacks in American life.

What he hoped for next was an opportunity to play an
active role in improving the situation of other blacks in the
United States, helping them to achieve social and economic
success in American society as he himself already had done.

Typical of Robinson, he had no intention of being content
to "wait till next year," as in competing for a World Series or
National League championship, to bring about changes for
people of his race. He intended to do it at once.

Bill Black, the owner of the Chock Full o'Nuts restaurant
chain, was a white man. Even before hiring Jackie Robinson,

however, he had made it a point to include many blacks among his employees. From the very beginning of his relationship with Jackie, Black gave the former baseball star much free time to work for improvements in racial relationships.

By the end of the 1960 presidential election campaign Robinson found himself deeply involved in national politics. In a move he later considered a serious mistake, he backed Republican Richard M. Nixon over the Democratic candidate, John F. Kennedy. At the time, however, he was deeply disappointed to find Kennedy far more interested in foreign affairs than in the plight of American black people.

In one conference, the future President Kennedy explained that he knew relatively little about problems of race. "Well . . . make it your business to meet Negroes, dammit!" exploded Jackie impatiently.

Nixon, on the other hand, while serving as vice-president under Dwight D. Eisenhower, had gone out of his way to please Robinson on racial matters.

In the years that followed, although removed from the action of the ball field, Jackie still felt very much a part of the game. In January 1962 he was thrilled to learn of his election to the Baseball Hall of Fame. Major national figures, including President Kennedy, wrote to congratulate him. Yet, at the time of his induction into the Hall at Cooperstown, New York, Robinson's special tributes went to his wife, his mother, and to Branch Rickey, all of whom were alive to celebrate that very special day of recognition for his success in the game.

In the years that followed, Jackie Robinson became involved in a wide variety of activities and causes. Once he stood up strongly against anti-Semitic acts in Harlem, focused especially on the Jewish owners of the famous Apollo Theater

Robinson and his wife, Rachel, with Branch Rickey at Robinson's 1962 induction into the Baseball Hall of Fame. *National Baseball Library & Archive, Cooperstown, New York*

on 125th Street. Intolerance, he declared, was *wrong*, whether it be against blacks or *by* blacks.

Similarly, he took a strong stand against Malcolm X, a leader of America's black Muslims. "I reject your racist views," he said. "I reject your dream of a separate state. . . . Thank God for our Dr. Bunche, our Roy Wilkins, [and] our Dr. King. . . ."

As Jackie Robinson grew older and more active in politics, he increasingly came to believe there were two keys to the advancement of blacks in America: "the ballot and the buck." What black people needed to do was organize themselves politically while at the same time becoming involved in manufacturing, job creation, and business development.

To achieve those ends he helped to organize the Freedom National Bank in Harlem. That institution received tremendous support from such well-known leaders as New York City's mayor, John V. Lindsay, and the governor of New York State, Nelson Rockefeller. Eventually, however, Robinson himself became disappointed in the bank's practices, considering his relationship with it "painful to relate."

Events in national politics also caused unhappiness for Robinson. In 1968 Richard Nixon's choice of the reportedly racist Spiro Agnew as a vice-presidential running mate very much disappointed him. Finally, the behavior of Nixon himself led Robinson to back the Democratic candidate, Hubert Humphrey.

Meanwhile, Robinson began to regret his initial defense of the war in Vietnam, where his own son had served in battlefront situations and become addicted to drugs. As Robinson put it, "I cannot accept the idea of a black supposedly fighting for the principles of freedom and democracy in Vietnam when so little has been accomplished in this country."

The continuing problems of race in America, along with even more depressing news from Vietnam, troubled him greatly. "There was a time when I deeply believed in America," he said. "Now, I have become bitterly disillusioned."

When Martin Luther King, Jr., was assassinated Robinson became even more gravely depressed. Looking around him, he saw hatred and brutality. To achieve the society Dr. King had in mind when he once proclaimed, "I have a dream," it now appeared to the former baseball star that Americans had "a long way to go."

It was at that time, too, that Robinson suffered a severe personal loss. His son, Jackie, Jr., who returned from Vietnam and left the army in 1967, soon afterward was arrested for carrying a concealed weapon. The problem was rooted in drug addiction, something the family fought hard to control, enrolling young Jackie in a narcotics rehabilitation program.

For a time it appeared the drug program was working. Then, one night in June 1971, when he was twenty-four years old, Jackie Robinson, Jr.'s automobile slammed into a heavy stone bridge support on a Connecticut highway, putting an end to his life.

At the funeral a group of young children came dressed in baseball uniforms, members of a local Jackie Robinson fan club. To a father shattered by the tragedy of his son's life and death, they were the symbol of a hope that someday the future might be better.

In 1965, Branch Rickey had died. To Jackie, he was the man who had helped make baseball "the most democratic of sports." Yet what Robinson still found missing were black men as managers and baseball executives. Since then, players such as outfielder Frank Robinson (not related to Jackie) have gone on to manage major league clubs, while former first baseman Bill White was chosen as president of the National League. At that time, however, Jackie declared impatiently that something should be done, or as he bluntly put it, "Baseball had better wake up!" Probably it was at least in part because of him that things finally did change.

As he grew older Robinson encountered more and more serious health problems: diabetes, high blood pressure, and a heart attack. But still, what bothered him most were matters relating to continued racial tension in the nation. His wife, Rachel, remembered how angry he once became after personally encountering a NO COLORED poster. As she described it, Jackie later took a bucket of golf balls and hit one after another into a nearby pond. It was Jackie himself who pointed out that the golf balls were white.

Gradually Robinson's eyesight failed. He continued to receive many letters from fans, but could not read them. Blindness seemed a very real danger. Once, Clyde Sukeforth, the coach who had first scouted him for Branch Rickey, came to see him at a special luncheon. Not until Sukeforth moved close enough to shake hands could Jackie even recognize him.

On October 24, 1972, Robinson arose to face the day. Almost immediately he collapsed with a heart attack. Before the ambulance carrying him ever reached the hospital, he had died.

Jackie Robinson personally opened the doorway to professional baseball for black people. That act, in turn, helped bring about such changes as desegregation in the nation's schools and workplaces, and more important roles for African Americans in politics. A fierce competitor, Robinson at first succeeded in holding in his sense of personal pride, ignoring taunts and insults, until he had proved his worth as a ballplayer, without regard to skin color.

Unlike others who wanted blacks to play an equal role in American society, Jackie Robinson was not willing to wait for the distant future. Instead, he hoped to speed up change. His pride, his courage, and his skills and daring as a ballplayer helped to achieve at last the goals he had in mind for people of his race.

The lessons of his life, however, go beyond the matter of race. He was a hero in a much broader sense—a hero for all of humanity. If his life proved anything, it was that a person of strength and will and with a vision of the future can apply himself and fulfill his dreams. He can also win respect.

Many other ballplayers, black and white, have hit more home runs than Robinson, have stolen more bases, have compiled higher batting averages. But it was Jackie Robinson whose triumph truly made a difference.

As a result of his effort, major league baseball undoubtedly is better today than before he appeared on the scene.

And so is the United States of America.

SOME CONCLUDING THOUGHTS

Ty Cobb.

Babe Ruth.

Jackie Robinson.

Three men who played important roles in shaping the game of baseball.

They were very different people, different in their values, different in their views of how life should be lived.

Yet they also were remarkably alike in certain ways. All three cared deeply about success. They wanted to win at the sport they were playing, wanted to stand out as individuals. All three took pride in what they were achieving and in the skills they displayed before great crowds of spectators.

It may well be that Babe Ruth was truly "born great," blessed with enormous natural ability that, both as a pitcher and a hitter of home runs, he simply polished and brought to bear, thus winning for himself everlasting fame.

It may be true, too, that Ty Cobb "achieved greatness" through hard work, intelligence, and remarkable daring.

There is little doubt that Jackie Robinson had "greatness thrust upon him," having been cast in the role of a talented athlete selected for the challenge of breaking the barrier of racial prejudice in professional baseball.

But William Shakespeare himself knew, when he wrote of people who were "born great . . . achieved greatness, and . . . had greatness thrust upon them," that human nature goes far beyond those categories.

Cobb, Ruth, and Robinson were complex, very different kinds of people. They lived their personal lives in different ways. They were treated differently by fans.

All three of them, however, had one common trait: a deep dedication to *do well* at what they were doing. Without that passionate commitment they would not stand out today at the very pinnacle of baseball history.

From such a lesson, and from the stories of their lives, there is much that all of us can learn.

FOR FURTHER READING

Many books are useful in learning about Ty Cobb, Babe Ruth, and Jackie Robinson.

For Ty Cobb, among the most important are two volumes by Cobb himself: *Busting 'Em and Other Stories* (New York: Edward J. Clode, 1914) and *My Life in Baseball: The True Record*, with Al Stumpf (Garden City, N.Y.: Doubleday, 1961). An especially useful biography is Charles Alexander's *Ty Cobb* (New York: Oxford University Press, 1984).

Numerous volumes have been written about Babe Ruth. See Ruth's autobiography (with Bob Considine), *The Babe Ruth Story* (New York: E. P. Dutton and Company, 1948), as well as *The Babe and I*, by Claire Hodgson Ruth and Bill Slocum (Englewood Cliffs, N.J.: Prentice-Hall, 1959). Especially informative is Robert W. Creamer's *Babe: The Legend Comes to Life* (New York: Simon & Schuster, 1974). Most insightful of all, perhaps, is *The Life That Ruth Built*, by Marshall Smelser (Lincoln: University of Nebraska Press, 1975).

Two autobiographies by Jackie Robinson are outstanding. The first of them, *Wait Till Next Year* (New York: Random House, 1960), is told through the eyes of co-author Carl T. Rowan. The other, *I Never Had It Made*, with Alfred Duckett (New York: Putnam, 1972), is narrated in the first person. For a truly memorable narrative summary of the times, with valuable observations about Robinson as a person, see Roger Kahn's *The Boys of Summer* (New York: Harper and Row, 1971).

In preparing this book, the following works on baseball history also have been particularly helpful—and enjoyable:

Alexander, Charles C. *Our Game*. New York: Holt, 1991.

Astor, Gerald. *The Baseball Hall of Fame*. New York: Prentice-Hall, 1985.

Connor, Anthony J. *Voices from Cooperstown*. New York: Macmillan, 1982.

Durso, Joseph. *Baseball and the American Dream*. St. Louis: The Sporting News, 1986.

Honig, Donald. *Baseball America: The Heroes of the Game and the Times of Their Glory*. New York: Macmillan, 1985.

Okrent, Daniel, and Harris Lewine, eds. *The Ultimate Baseball Book*. Boston: Houghton Mifflin, 1979.

INDEX

Page numbers for illustrations are in *italics*